REMEMBER MY GRAVE

TWO FACES

SUMEET KUMAR

Made with ♥ on the Notion Press Platform
www.notionpress.com

SUMEET KUMAR

SUMEET KUMAR , A adult who experinces many phases of life , a well known writer and a writer of new era .In reality he is a writer as well as ,singer ,poeter ,shayr ,quote writer ,lyric writer and and a performer well as anchor or standup comedian.Very exicting and intresting fact about him is that he is author of new era i.e. He starts his journey of writing at the age when he was going to schools to get the study .His streak of 200 books will be the great achievment for him in future ,His some famous works i.e Maturity of love (genre _Love) Privacy of dream (Genre -LIFE STYLE OF MIDDLE CLASS).

you can also buy his book from NOTION PRESS ,ABE BOOKS ,IMUSIC IN ,FLIPKART ,AMAZON ,KINDLE ,INSTANT READ LIKE EBOOK ,KINDLE ,GOOGLE ,INTERNATIONAL SITES AND MANY

MORE .

PODCASTER ON SPOTIFY :@BROKEN HEART

INSTA ID : BOOKHUB92

GMAIL: sumitkumar 88234

LINKEDIAN : SUMEET KUMAR

.

Contents

Preface

Friendship is that wish of life which gives someone the courage to live, but if it becomes poison, it gives a grave to a person while alive this is not just a story, it is the beginning of a happy life that I have lived in hope of deception.

Atul Chaurisaya I don't know how long my life will hold me ,because the one who has given his life to death has traded my life so many times that now even death considers me as his lover.

Acknowledgements

SUMEET KUMAR

SUMEET KUMAR , A adult who experinces many phases of life , a well known writer and a writer of new era .In reality he is a writer as well as ,singer ,poet ,quote writer ,lyric writer and and a performer well as anchor or standup comedian.Very exicting and intresting fact about him is that he is author of new era i.e. He starts his journey of writing at the age when he was going to schools to get the study .His streak of 200 books will be the great achievment for him in future ,His some famous works i.e Maturity of love (genre _Love) Privacy of dream (Genre -LIFE STYLE OF MIDDLE CLASS).

you can also buy his book from NOTION PRESS ,ABE BOOKS ,IMUSIC IN ,FLIPKART ,AMAZON ,KINDLE ,INSTANT READ LIKE EBOOK ,KINDLE ,GOOGLE

ACKNOWLEDGEMENTS

,INTERNATIONAL SITES AND MANY MORE .
   PODCASTER ON SPOTIFY :@BROKEN HEART
   INSTA ID : BOOKHUB92
   GMAIL: sumitkumar 88234
   LINKEDIAN : SUMEET KUMAR

   .

CHAPTER ONE

IMMORTAL THESIS

Everyone's story is not immortal and crazy they never express and do not love because what they think is never requested to be in their part, if I say in simple words then life is like that color film There is a party to see which has to be done at many stakes, everyone is in public but no one believes that what is this life in the end,
When the destination is close and the path is different, then at that time we do not understand whose hope is it. For example, life is also a gamble, if I tell the truth, because its addresses are never the same, and those who have the same as they have, people say God, meaning the one above, they believe that our lives are in their hands, but There is someone who does not even know that in whose hands his life is, this story is also of the same witness about whom my words are a bit crude.

And be sure, well, before his story, at least be aware of life, sir, because nowadays we are far away and unconsciously, I have given a custom of giving coffins, but I do not know much about life. I also know that it is enough, I have spent my whole life in this question that what is my life missing from me? I know that the bell in your mind has rung long ago, and you all must be finding my thinking a bit different.

And many people would consider me crazy too, but it is not such a thing at all, what I want to write is to say that its path may be right or not but the destination can never be wrong, this life is a journey and we are its Mushfir hai is everyone's words which they use because of their words, but my upbringing is not different from all of them because neither I am a traveler nor my life is a journey. I just know that my today

The statue is very different from my yesterday, and Ishi is called life, when you think about yourself and work hard for your today, love him, time never changes, he only changes his condition, his life too there is someone who forgets his past by getting stuck in past and future, I always talk about life because apart from this

There is nothing else in our journey with which we can consider ourselves worthy, I don't know if this story of mine will lead to distance from me at the last moment, but I definitely know that if it started with me Sayyed aunt will be loved by my soul, then it is clear that today I will do everything, but the flame of trust Has tried to hurt love in that way which I can't reveal my condition to anyone, this is not only my story but also of all those who are trying to handle themselves, that too after breaking many times. Later, but their condition is forcing them every day, even today there are some memories which bother me throughout the night, there are some houses whose Ugly sisters haunt me even today.

CHAPTER TWO

BLUR PART OF LIFE

I want to go away from them, but now it is not possible because every brick in the wall was built in the relationships of those houses, now every brick has become stronger than me, and I can tell them Can't break, there is no story of a man, everyone says that he is a very helpless character, does not accept life as easy, but who said this? Who is a helpless person, doesn't his tears fall, doesn't he have that above Make? Doesn't it feel small Isn't it a human? Ish Samaj has many questions and no answer, I have lost people's arguments and listen to dogs because their words have become the reason for the wrong method of this society , their thinking is also as weak as their society, The society which does not understand the condition of a man, for the sake of that society is exactly like that person who only prays for death and does not suppress it, well this fight was never mine, I never did it .

I never thought that I will do something like too, I will also write something like that , I myself do not even know how long this journey is, I myself am a traveler in those abuses where every path is very unknown to me, like this story no human being at all, because neither his words nor his words struck me in the slightest when I met him? And if it is the same then it ruins the relationship, when we go close to someone, we never think that what they are for us for this, whatever is important to the public is very important and do not know, after a time, we make them so close to us that even after saying this, we can never erase their memories from our heart and after that we ourselves This is a minor thing that you will see in every journey these days, I am not saying these things to you, these are old things, but the pain still seems new, do this we cannot feel pain because it is a the name of time is very different from others, everyone must have heard it.

CHAPTER THREE

GIFT OF DEVIL

Because this is the gift of life which if it is found on the right date then it looks like spring of flowers in the house and if it is not found then it will be bitten, how much should I express my pain I used to think earlier because this life is the name of reducing the pain. Only taking After all, to whom should I ask the story of peace, because nowadays I am bereft of every life, Relationships do not stay together by spending time, they stay together when you

We are together, people ask me a big question these days, what kind of desire that you lost in life, because of which they call her an ocean of pain, in words, what should I say to her that I have passed through in which gathering alot of uncertified memories , I have also passed through a pain which was gathering inside me. and yeah he seems to be bereft of the memories of gatherings, I don't know but people often become poets in love, even if their words are not right but their pain is clearly visible, there will definitely be a request to God that if they If I have a match, then I ask in prostration that God suppresses the trouble, otherwise he may take away the life that he has given from me, it is said that when we move towards a destination, then there are many ways to go, but where to go, no one knows, Because if the way is clear with gathering then the blessings of pain go to the weak and so much hope it will not cross the back, and if it goes to the weak by mistake then the blessings of time make it even stronger, this life also of that weather thread It is the kind that sometimes gives courage to even a cut kite to fly in the sky, but if it is dedicated hard work, I want to identify myself in my life, I know that I am a man, but does the society also ask for the same in us, they test our near and dear ones like a stone.

They were also ignorant about life, just like me, means my story is also related to him, but for me he is nothing special.

CHAPTER FOUR

THE JOURNEY OF GOD

Because I never understood it, my exceptional pain of life is the only part of my life whom I never want to forget because she is like a friend to me, and a person can forget the charity given from far away, but he never forgets the charity given by himself, my existence.

Every story is related to him, but he is neither my own nor I am a stranger to him, the story of love is false and true, but its words are the truth of the same dream that we see everyday in our shadow, love every bit of the story Before keeping I want to say something about myself, my place is not what they understand, my place is what I want to explain to them, that too God's journey, I am the end of God's story, not the beginning. Well I know that I can't support him till the end, still some things which I am writing in my own words in the support of God's story, if there is any desire, then my words must be brought in front of him once in a while.

CHAPTER FIVE

BIG WAIST

Because the big waist in a human being gave me the courage to understand my own condition which even my aunt could not give me, even though we are not related by blood relation, but when every wish of her is Gujarati through my gathering, then like that I have a feeling that he is for me, to the extent that everyone must have understood my story, because what I want to say, I am saying that he is my own, but he does not know these things and I knew before time, they say when relationship is unknown then love is also unknown, but When he becomes aware of his relationship with himself, then every limit of him seems easy, I cannot reveal to anyone what I lost, but whatever I lost was very precious, whenever I remember it, I myself I can't handle it, and then later I think that what mistake have I made in life that even though it is in my part, it is away from me. I just want to tell you that if we get life again, we will play with each other again in the same house.

Where we ask for our home, we run in the same abuses where the charity is still there like our memories. I don't leave you, whenever you need me, call me, don't be afraid, my brother, even though I have made thousand promises with you, but that God had written our fate separately, I don't know who is with me in my last time. Who is not, but can definitely say this much Yes, even if I die in prostration, I will pass through your shoulders. Well if my story is over then you are the hero of the film , and in the world such a film has been made in ghost work, in which the heroes give their lives, but Ish never spoke like this in the film because I will be your own. I am going after doing handed my illusion , so be careful with me and yourself too.

CHAPTER SIX

TROUBLE FIGHT

Friendship, this is all that we use in life when our life becomes such a murky pier where the path is visible but the destination is a bit hazy, I am writing this today after losing everything, I agree that my Relationships have become weak, my life is also nothing special now, but what is the beginning of my aunt, this is the evening of a new dawn, when life

She also changes by staying with us, we don't even know, the pain in which I am writing Akaj started long ago, today there are only memories of her who is imprisoned in my house, I have never befriended anyone in my life. But when he spoke to someone with full devotion, he never made himself weak in front of them, because if people knew that he was in my happiness.

If he is involved then he will definitely be in sorrow, but these are only the things of that world which we do not know well and will never be able to be aware of, because the world is in his heart; May you be lucky, people ask many questions in a day, that too to the one above, but do they ask as many questions to themselves, this same request to themselves, I don't think so because as far as I have seen people close to me they only think about themselves, mandir ,Mosques are just excuses and that too to complete their own work, have we ever asked that almighty how are you? How is your life going? Are you in trouble? But what happened suddenly? And why did it happen? I retraced my steps at that time and that too helped him.

CHAPTER SEVEN

ADOPT AND DESTROY

Maybe that my life is that night, in which I could not forget till date, it is not a matter of luxury that I am not trying to forget, but I am not able to forget, why that God has made me like God, now I also ask that question. I have stopped doing it, because whenever I see a poor people in front of me, who has neither the thread of Rakhi nor the touch of slippers in her feet, then at that time I forget what I have lost in my life. ?And what do I want to get for myself going forward?

There are some words that stand for those relationships that support someone because they have a lot of wealth and also fear, I am saying these things because I have gone through this time, I have gone through those relationships. In the beginning, we used to look like our own, but when the intensity of time and silence woke up, they became strangers in a moment, what I feel every day, they are ignorant of God, my life is shaped like a wall They don't even know that it has happened, but yes there are some things

What I know about them but I never had the courage to tell them that each and every aspect of your love is heavy with deceit, you cannot adopt me because because of you I will never get that night which gives me peace. I don't know why you want to destroy me, but if I become an inhabitant of the street, I will destroy your race, by the way, these things are related to my condition, in which I have conspired to make myself conscious then, and When did his condition come, when did the memories ruin me, these will only take you all towards my destination on the way forward.

26\05\1987

Lucknow

Heaven Valley Apartment

226001

Pancham Nagar..

Date: 26\05\1987

26 \ 05 \ 1987, this is a minor day to be missed because on this day every beginning of my life which has been drenched in the rain of sorrow from my happiness, does not mean that every impression of my birth is on this day ,It is related to the day when even the reception of happiness was like death on my part., friendship is getting life on one side and I am saying love in these things because the friendship which ,I don't know if I will tell my God story completely to all of you or not, I don't even know if I will write the end of God story It is not because my desires are taking me away from myself, they say that sorrows heal with time but deception never heals,, Their shocks are so harsh, that you will not be able to remove it from yourself even by saying it, because in life we take those sorrows which we get in the relationship, but those sorrows which we get in friendship, even that I don't have silence only for me, it can be replaced by death, can it be? 1987, when two flowers bloom in the same house Can control but when

they grow up and have some understanding then they don't even like to see each other and similar is the story of me and my friend, I don't want to reveal his name nor I want to defame my friendship, but how can I forget the last gift of the pain those relationships gave me?

DEPARTURE OF WAR

"AFTER MY
DEPARTURE
YOU MAY OR
MAY NOT
REMEMBER ME
BUT GOD BLESS
WHOEVER
YOU STAY WITH
SHOULD LOVE
LIKE ME ....."

CHAPTER TEN

ANGEL BECOME DEVIL

Fahad Qureshi, this identity may be unknown to all of you, but for me it is not unknown at all, nor can I ever forget him, because if there is any desire to identify my pain, Ishi's name is behind it. , But are you all saying so much? I haven't even composed the story yet, well I talk a lot, it is my habit which was there before and may be even today?

Fahad Qureshi is the name with whom I have shared my childhood, I have seen every evening with this person which was a bit cruel to me and also comforting, both me and Fahad belonged to different religions and everyone knows these things. But before that, they definitely knew about us that even though their religions may be different, their paths will always be the same, even though our families were different, and the identity of our religion and their rituals were different. But they say religion in friendship ,caste t has also accepted love, we have never thought of what religion we belong to Whenever he calls me, he used to run away leaving everything, I also remember those nights when he cried holding my hand for the first time and I was in it at that time that I saw my friend say whatever happens in life, we Even if we don't stay together in the future, but this promise to you ,I promise that I will not leave your side, and this is Atul Chaurasia's promise that if the common man does not, then you now shut up and let me show you a film and you know what the name of that film is." Pushpa I Hate Tears ".

CHAPTER ELEVEN

BETRYAL WITH LOVE

I still don't know where he had so much hatred for me, this love, but I know for sure that I have ever looked at him in such a way that he would hate me, I have never done anything wrong like that our friendship should be scared. Whenever I used to sit silent, he used to make me laugh in one way or the other, we didn't just grow up together, our birth dates were also the same, that means the magic that God does in a thousand years, just like ours magic of birth date It was done on the same day, that too one houses, don't understand the meaning, means we both have the same date of birth, and it means that both of us entered the divine world at the same time, that too under the same terrace, Only the rooms were different.

At that time that doctor did not even know what name should I give to this magic, because sometimes he used to say congratulations on one side and on the other side, I had only heard earlier that the world is round, but I did not know that it was so round. These are not my words, they belong to that doctor, at that time there was a friendship between my father and Fahd's father, and from that day till a few days ago, both of us were living a very good life, but in the time of betrayal, only his Want to know the reason?

CHAPTER TWELVE

17 YEARS

For 17 years our life was simple, means we play together, talk, then go to school together, and even if I used to go to mosque and he to temple with me, whenever we see people together So it is said that look "Jai" Veeru "couple has come out on Sakdo, the world used to get jealous seeing our strong relationship and I always used to talk to him and he used to say at that time that no matter what the world does, this is something Also say that I will not leave your side nor

I will never cheat on you , but it is said that humans only talk, maintain relationships, when the silence of time surrounds them, then they appear with their real self. Kept away and kept that relationship safe. When the first fear came, I had lost it at the same time, I don't know what I was feeling at that time, but there was definitely a name in the eyes and there was such a feeling inside the heart. was the one who ruined anyone Could have been, and he does not even tell how this situation happened because these things were not special for me at that time but how they became special for Fahad, at that time I was not even aware of it, so sir, the matter is such that the 12th board All of us were very nervous thinking about the result coming, I mean all our schoolmates who were close to me. Those who are going to fail on that time should be nervous.

PROGRESS BECOME POISON

I thought that let's go, whatever will happen will be seen, I was chilling comfortably in love, but in no time our results also came. Anything else, Jaysheh is behaving exactly like Devdas. When my results came, the percentage numbers we got were almost 99%89, so BJ went to share his happiness with Fahad, and when he went,so we had not even seen our result, so I also did not say anything to him about my result, he also asked me what has happened to you? I told him at that time also that I will see my friend, let's see your result first. maybe it was wrong that day, my life was going wrong for Fahad that day, because friendship means a life where you are relaxed. There are nights of celebration and evenings of celebration, my and Fahadh's friendship is like this before that day.

But when Fahad saw his result, he had failed in two subjects, and you all must be thinking that if their friendship is about to break, then sayyyed, this would be the reason? But I haven't said anything yet, Ayesha, but the vibe is of the same thing isn't it, when Fahad's eyes went to his result, he had become so silent at that time that I had not even thought about it, I mean at that time I am voicing that there must have been some mistake on the part of the boards by worrying Fahad, and your will challenge for the board's paper, I didn't know how he was feeling at that time, but I definitely knew that he needed me, but I would have handled it earlier, my happiness at the same time raised his hopes. I didn't know when will I build the walls of silence, it is said that when everything is going on in life, some relationships always take care of us, that day when I was in Fahad's room and was explaining to him, at that time PT Sir's Entered, and happened ,he directly told me that I don't want to hug Topper sir, even after that he didn't stop and there were many other things, and those things were something like this, I had already expected that you are the best, but I am so much better. I didn't know that your head is not only the pride of our school but also the pride of my PT uncle, I want to say that I am your PT sir, but I am your father's friend first and I am proud that you are my friend's son.

CHAPTER FOURTEEN

FIND MY BROTHER

Hearing his words that day for the first time, I wish I would not have got this victory in him because on one hand the silence of Fahad which was not taking the name of leaving at that time and on the other hand the happiness of PT uncle which I did not like at that time. And the reason behind it was that my friend was silent, before this I tried to control him, only one voice was echoing in the whole neighborhood that I have topped my school, even Fahad's father and mother should encourage me. were living But at that time it was definitely known that Fahad needs me and I should be with him, he was with me at that time when PT uncle came to our room, but all the people started shouting at me, I didn't know where I went, I didn't meet him at that very foggy time, I went to the terrace, I went to the park where we often used to play, even I went to the ghost house where we both used to play hiden seek , but i didn't find it there either I was upset after that, I was feeling that he might do something wrong with me, and this would have happened if I had not met him on time.

CHAPTER FIFTEEN

FIGHT FOR GRAVE

It is said that friendship is never possible with the same people and it is not possible to love because there are many reasons behind it, which I cannot try to blur even by saying this, because if I start looking for it, I will go to the grave. Night can be very soon in my part, I have asked something from the Almighty for my life and It's not that he didn't give me time, whenever I used to return empty handed at his door, my bag was always full, I don't know exactly how important Fahad was to me, but if I tell the truth I had not seen life without water, but how did I know that my life would be poisoned in my life, see today something like this ,I am going to tell you facts about friendship, which I can never say otherwise, because today every one of its feelings is imprisoned inside me and in which I will definitely come out, friendship can never become love, nor can it always be with you like the flame of relationships. Will remain, friend means two unknown people who only need each other, I can not say that friends are not real in the world, I mean to say that the way this world has become sweetly formed, in the same way its relationships have also become formed, and they have become so much that you can say their nature. Can't erase, I am writing these things because I have gone through a phase and I don't know about the world but I definitely know that every relationship is not true and we cannot adopt every human being as humanity.

,

CHAPTER SIXTEEN

Sudama's fate

Everyone must have heard the story of the great Sudama and Lord Krishna, it was not that Lord Krishna did not know about their condition, he knew about the whole universe, so how could he not know the condition of his friends, but All of you must have thought that if such a thing did not happen before, why did not he help them because he was waiting for so long.Why were there, there is neither any charity that I will try to measure to everyone and I have no words, but yes I can definitely say that even after knowing that if she was silent then understand that she was in so much trouble, Even though he came on the earth in the form of a human being, but when he met Sudama, he became a humble person that day, for his friends, if he had said, he could have removed all their sorrows long ago, But if he had helped his friend long ago

If he had done it, he would never have become maybe , which was written in Sudama's fate.

Charity Of Life

A person can fight with his relations but never with his fate, and this charity was written in my part that day, I went to find the lost friend in the mist, I got such a cuff from him, even after saying that I I will not be able to get away from myself that day, and I can't do it because the cuff that I got in his share, the one who got the nadaulat was none other than Fahd, means that day when I saw the prayer of hatred for myself in his eyes. , then at the same time ,my soul said goodbye to me and I could not bring her to me even after saying it, but what happened that day ? the friendship which I considered bigger than my relationships, at last she became poison for me in a moment. .

When I went out to wash him, he did not show me anywhere, I mean to say that wherever we both used to go, he used to wash me at the same place, not only me but also PT uncle and Fahad and my parents also saw him. Had gone to sleep, because by that time everyone had a feeling that Fahad was not well, we all searched for him first in our building, then in the park, and then in that ghostly bangle which I have mentioned. Even then we did not get it, at that time I I was very upset, I could not understand what should I do? On the one hand, there was such happiness that it was not more important than my friend, and I did not have that feeling at that time, there were tears in my eyes at that time, but to whom was there no one to tell me that I do not want anything? , I want my best friend. We all were very worried that day, we were feeling that no accident should happen to Fahad, he should not do something to himself, that's why we thought that before this many If it gets late then we should complain to the police station and everyone was getting ready to go together when Fahad comes in the same distance, and he had some gifts with him, I don't know what it was but he had brought something, well like Even when he came, we all had only one question on our lips, and that was where he had gone for so long, what was he doing? Even if he went, why didn't he go by telling how upset we all were, he used to say something to him earlier, why did he go to the mosque ?

Lost In The Arms Of Betray

For Atul because today is a big day for him, and it was my fault that I had left my phone at home, and I fell in love a little too long because I had stopped to buy cake for him. What says why did you tell me all this? What makes me angry with him? That heart has won the hearts of the people At that time he did what I would never be able to do, but it is said that behind every smile there is another breed hidden, the world could see his good intentions that day and I too, but behind him was the love of my fan. I didn't know that she was going to come, and before that I tried to leave her, before that the writings of my existence had already prepared to be erased, when we were celebrating, I went to that Fahad went because I

Had to talk to him and at that time he went by saying to everyone that Fahad is up in front of him, Ishqiye, everyone said that Fahad is up, in love. I went upstairs to meet him and talk to him, but before that he also went upstairs and fell unconscious on the third floor.

That's why I didn't fall on the stairs at that time But I didn't even know how it happened, means it happened to me for the first time, and everyone heard the sound of my fall, they all came running, they thought that Fahad had done something, they Seeing me everyone started itching that what happened till now it was fine, but the thing to do in hair was that Fahad did not come to see me even at that time, I even asked everyone that where is Fahad? But everyone said that now he will be on maybe Terrace, well you

Leave him, take care of yourself, many things were unknown that day and seemed unknown to me, first of all,

Fahad knew that I do not like cake at all, I am allergic to it, yet he specially made it for me. Another surprising thing is that Fahad never used to go to the mosque on Fridays, even my family members did not know about me as much as they did, why did we do this? They used to say are not in friendship.

Last Journey With New Begining

Even if poison is given instead of celebration, it seems like nectar, I knew that I am allergic to cake, yet I ate it because Fahad had brought that cake, and that too for me, my family never knew this I wasn't allergic to cakes, how will I know the last time he is not with me all the time, I took everything very lightly on a good day, but the next day my health was even worse, I had to face my family take to the hospital Gone, but the way my eyes were silent everywhere in the search, he did not come, when the doctors did my checkup, then the thing that came to the fore was shocking, and that thing was such that it poisoned me. Was gone, and that poison was like that if it is not treated with time, then the death of a person is also a power, and if we talk about its effect, then after a day, it neither allows a person to live well nor Who gave me that poison when I died?

I was neither in such a condition at that time that I could doubt anyone, I should go after that criminal who has made me in this situation, they say that when someone's story comes on such a path, when it comes, then the faces are clear. Otherwise, at that time there is a great need for us to remain a saint, but at that time I was very scared for the first time and it was not love that I was about to die, it was a dying child, the love I was thinking of, if only it was not? Whose hand is behind everything, this is the one I am thinking about, may it not be him.

And he is no one else, I am talking about Fahad only, this story is not over yet because it is clear that he is coming, but he also has two faces towards today's relationships and there are two ways too, now let's see my

destination gives me death yet a kind of life , this deception
in it?